OWEN FOOTE, SUPER SPY

OWEN FOOTE, SUPER SPY

by STEPHANIE GREENE

illustrated by MARTHA WESTON

CLARION BOOKS • NEW YORK

For Cooper and Alyssa,
who taught me a thing or two
—S. G.

For Peter
—M. W.

Clarion Books
a Houghton Mifflin Company imprint
215 Park Avenue South, New York, NY 10003
Text copyright © 2001 by Stephanie Greene
Illustrations copyright © 2001 by Martha Weston

The text was set in 13.5-point Palatino.
The illustrations were executed in pencil.

www.houghtonmifflinbooks.com

Printed in the U.S.A.

Library of Congress Cataloging-in-Publication Data

Greene, Stephanie.
Owen Foote, super spy / by Stephanie Greene ; illustrated by Martha Weston.
p. cm.
Summary: Owen and his friends decide that spying on the
school principal at his own house will be a fun challenge.
ISBN 0-618-11752-0
[1. Spies—Fiction. 2. Honesty—Fiction. 3. School principals—Fiction.
4. Friendship—Fiction. 5. Humorous stories.] I. Weston, Martha, ill. II. Title.
PZ7.G8434 Oyf   2001
[Fic]—dc21   00060341
CIP
AC

MV 10 9 8 7 6 5 4

CONTENTS

1

"What *Are* You Doing?"

"Dad will never see me."

"Owen?" said Mrs. Foote. She sounded amazed. "What *are* you doing?"

Owen walked toward the kitchen table. He had on his too-big green fishing vest with a million pockets, a green T-shirt, and green pants. On his head, he was wearing his new camouflage headgear.

"Are those Dad's boxer shorts?" said his mom.

"They had a hole in them," said Owen. He shifted the headgear up so that the eyeholes were over his eyes again and not his nose. He didn't want to trip and ruin how cool he looked. "Dad won't care."

Mr. Foote's white boxer shorts were covered with dabs of dark green and light green paint. There were brown dabs, too, and a strip of bright red around the top.

Two empty leg holes flopped down over Owen's ears.

"Isn't it great?" he said. "If we were outside right now, you could hardly see me."

Owen whipped the shorts off his head and put them on the table in front of his mother. "Pretty realistic, huh?"

His mom didn't say anything. But from the way her eyebrows were raised high above her eyes, Owen could tell she was impressed.

"Is that the waistband?" she said finally. She pointed to the strip of red elastic.

Owen nodded. "I cut it off and sewed it on top to hold the thing on, but it keeps slipping down. I have to sew it tighter."

He slipped the shorts over his head again and stared out at her. "I'm going to try it out on Dad."

"Do I see what I think I see?"

Lydia, Owen's sister, was standing in the

kitchen door with a horrified expression on her face. "Are those Dad's boxer shorts?"

"Lydia . . ." warned their mom.

"I can't stand it." Lydia staggered into the kitchen and fell into a chair as if she had been mortally wounded. "My brother's wearing underwear on his head."

She raised her hands to the ceiling. "Why me?" she cried. "Why am I the only person in the world who has Owen for a brother?" She put her head down on her arms and made loud sobbing noises.

Mrs. Foote started to laugh.

"It's not funny, Mom," said Owen. The eyeholes slipped down over his cheeks and nose again. "Darn!" He whipped the camouflage off. "I can't get this thing tight enough."

"You know what the worst thing about this is, Owen?" said Lydia. "You think it's perfectly normal. You don't see anything wrong with wearing your father's underwear on your head. You think everyone does. And if they don't, you think they should."

"Lydia, that's enough." Mrs. Foote put her

hand on Owen's shoulder. "I'm sorry I laughed, Owen. It's really very creative. But why did you paint the waistband red? Doesn't that defeat the whole purpose of camouflage?"

"It's supposed to be like the property line."

His mom looked blank.

"You know the red tape they tie around trees to mark a property line?" Owen said. "That's how they marked the line at the house Mr. Gallo's building. Joseph and me are going to spy on the builders, so I painted the waistband the same color."

"Joseph and I," said Mrs. Foote.

"You're going out in *public* like that?" said Lydia.

"That way, if they see me move," said Owen, ignoring her, "they'll think it's the property line."

"The *moving* property line?" Lydia shook her head, as if every new word out of Owen's mouth was more incredible than the one before. "I can't believe what I'm hearing."

"If this thing works the way I think it will," said Owen, "I can probably sell some to the government."

"Right, Owen. That's what this country really needs," said Lydia. "The CIA walking around with recycled underwear on their heads."

Mrs. Foote went and stood in front of the sink. They could see her shoulders shaking.

"It's not funny, Mom," Lydia said indignantly. "When you laugh like that, you only encourage him."

"You two don't know anything," Owen said disgustedly. "You should try spying sometime. It's the coolest thing in the world."

"I'm sorry, Owen." His mom turned around to face him. "It's just that sometimes you amaze me. You really do."

"He's always been like this," said Lydia. "Remember when he was little? He used to come into the room and put his hands over his eyes and say, 'You can't see me.' When he was standing right there, in plain sight."

"I did?" said Owen. "What a weirdo."

"You were such a comical little boy," said Mrs. Foote.

"Well, he's not that little anymore," Lydia said

grimly. "You have to make him stay inside when he's wearing that, Mom, or we'll be the laughing-stock of the whole town."

"Are you joking?" Owen snatched his head-gear off the table in case Lydia tried to grab it. "I spent a lot of time working on this thing. I can hardly wait to put it into action."

"What are you hoping to see the builders do?" said his mom.

"I don't know." Owen shrugged. "Stuff."

"You'll see stuff, all right," said Lydia. "You'll see them falling off their ladders, they'll be laugh-ing so hard."

"You wait," said Owen. "I'm good. I spied on Dad last weekend when he was working in his garden. I was about three feet away, and he never even knew I was there."

"When Dad's working in his garden, a space-ship could land next to him and he wouldn't notice it," Lydia said.

Lydia was right. It was very annoying.

"Oh, yeah? Well, what about yesterday?" he said. "When you were baby-sitting the Sweets. *I* saw what happened."

"Something happened at the Sweets'?" said Mrs. Foote.

"No. He's making it up."

"I am, am I?" Owen raised both eyebrows.

"Lydia, why didn't you tell me?" Their mom sounded worried.

"Because nothing happened," said Lydia. She tucked her hair behind her ears.

Good. Owen smirked. She's getting mad.

Lydia glared at Owen through slitty eyes. "Tell her, Owen," she said.

"Ohhhh, no." Owen waved his hands in front of his face as if he didn't want any part of the trouble Lydia was about to get into. "*I'm* not going to be the one to tell her."

"Would someone please tell me what happened at the Sweets'!" yelled Mrs. Foote.

"Gee, Mom, calm down," Owen said. "Nothing happened. But if it had"—he slipped his head-gear back on—"Owen Foote, Super Spy, would have seen it."

"I told you he was lying!" Lydia made a lunge for him, but Mrs. Foote caught her by her shoulders. Owen stepped neatly behind his mother.

"Make him apologize!" Lydia shouted. Her arms were flailing away on either side of her mother, trying to connect with a small piece of Owen. Mrs. Foote kept a firm grip.

Owen ducked around to the other side of the table. "Apologize for what? I didn't do anything."

"Calm down. Go back upstairs and finish your homework." Mrs. Foote was pushing Lydia gently but firmly out of the kitchen and toward the stairs. "I'll take care of Owen."

"I'll get you for this!" Lydia yelled.

"Go on." Their mom stood at the bottom of the stairs like a sentry to make sure Lydia went all the way to the top.

"Wait till they see you in Dad's underwear! They'll laugh you right out of town!"

Lydia's bedroom door slammed.

His mom came back into the kitchen and gave Owen a level stare. "Why do you have to get her worked up like that?"

"She makes fun of me, I get her in trouble," said Owen. "If you ask me, I think she has a guilty conscience." He started for the back door. "See you later."

"Owen, stop for a minute."

Owen stopped and turned around.

"I'm not sure it's a good idea for you and Joseph to spy on the Gallo house," said his mom. "Mr. Gallo might not like it."

"It's fine," said Owen. "He's Anthony's uncle. Anthony's going to come with us."

He opened the back door. "Besides, no one is going to see us, remember?"

"Well, be careful. I'd hate to see you get into trouble. And, sweetie?"

"What?"

His mom smiled. "Don't worry about what Lydia said. I think you look very nice."

"I do?" Owen's face fell.

He closed the door behind him. Great. The last thing he wanted was to look "nice."

If this thing looked "nice," it was coming off.

Owen peered into the rearview mirror on his dad's car. What was she talking about? he thought with relief. He didn't look nice.

He looked like a forest. Just the way he had planned. Sometimes his mom didn't have a clue.

Owen started to inch his way along the side of

the house toward the back yard. He could tell his mom thought he was crazy to think people might do things that were worth spying on. She thought everyone was normal, that no one ever did anything strange or weird.

Owen knew better.

One time, he and Joseph had spied on the Lees, the people who lived next door to Joseph. They were out on their porch with their baby. It looked like a sack of potatoes with a bowling ball on top, as far as Owen could see. But the way Mr. and Mrs. Lee were bouncing it up and down and making goo-goo noises at it, you would have thought it was the most wonderful thing in the world.

It was a pretty boring thing to spy on. He and Joseph were just about to leave when the baby did the most amazing thing. It threw up, straight out, like water out of a squirt gun.

Vomit hit Mrs. Lee right in the chest.

The way Mr. and Mrs. Lee both froze—with their mouths and eyes wide open—had made Owen and Joseph laugh so hard they'd fallen over each other all the way back to the house.

That was what spies lived for, Owen thought

now as he neared the corner of the house. To see someone normal do something incredible.

What was incredible depended on whom he was spying on, of course. Say he was spying on his dad, and his dad burped. That wouldn't be so amazing. His dad burped all the time.

And he wouldn't want to see his mom do something gross like pick her nose. It would be incredible, all right, but even thinking about his own mom doing something disgusting like that made him feel funny.

As for a little kid picking his nose, that was out, too. Little kids picked their noses all the time. Lots of them even ate it, like it was food.

Owen peered cautiously around the corner of the house. Great! His dad was talking to Mr. Bailey, their next-door neighbor. Sneaking up on two people who were talking definitely would be more challenging than sneaking up on one person who was in a trance.

He crouched down and made a dash for the apple tree in the side yard. He reached it and flattened his body against the trunk. He almost expected to hear bullets whizzing by, it felt so exciting.

When he was sure his dad hadn't seen him, he made a dash for another tree. He was so close now he could hear the rumble of their voices.

This was so cool. Maybe he would hear them say something important. Maybe his dad would say, "I think Owen's a genius," or "We've decided to buy Owen a dirt bike for his birthday."

The smell of paint was strong in his nostrils. The jagged edges of the underwear were blurry lines out of the corner of his eyes.

He felt invisible.

Unfortunately, he wasn't. Like a spy's worst nightmare, Major, his dog, came charging around the corner of the house.

Owen froze.

Major pounced on a yellow tennis ball lying in the grass. He tossed it up in the air. He rolled over on the ground and scratched his back against the grass. He flipped back over onto his feet.

Then he looked straight at Owen.

Owen did his best to look like a tree, but it was no good. Major came bounding across the yard

and made a flying leap right for him. He put his
paws on Owen's chest. He panted his smelly dog
breath in Owen's face.

"Down, boy!" Owen whispered. He pushed on
Major's head. "Down!"

Major's tail was wagging so hard it was as if he
hadn't seen Owen in a hundred years. Owen
picked up a stick and threw it as hard as he could.

Major went after it.

Owen peered out from behind the tree. His dad
was leaning on his rake, talking. Mr. Bailey had
his head bent, listening. Owen dropped to his

knees and scrambled closer behind an azalea bush.

"I used to use 5-10-5," he heard his dad say. "Then I switched to 15-30-15."

"15-30-15? I'll have to give it a try," said Mr. Bailey. "I use 30-30-30 on our flowers. Our peonies are as big as footballs."

Owen groaned.

Fertilizer. He should have known. His dad could talk about fertilizer for hours. There was a race in their house to see who could get out of the room fastest when his dad got on the subject of fertilizer.

Owen was almost glad when Major came running back. He dropped the stick in Owen's lap and stood there waiting for more. Owen scratched him behind his ears.

"Sorry to break this up, John," Mr. Bailey said suddenly, "but I've got to take Allison to the dentist."

Thank heavens for Allison and her rotten teeth! thought Owen. He pushed Major's head off his lap and got up onto his knees.

Mr. Bailey was walking away across his lawn. Mr. Foote was bending down to pick up the watering can. "Hi, Owen," he said. He didn't turn around.

Darn!

Owen pulled off his camouflage and stood up. "How long did you know I was there?"

"Since Major started attacking the tree. I figured he had either become an avid arborist or you were hiding behind it."

"I was practicing my spy techniques," said Owen. "I made it all the way across the yard without your knowing."

He balled his camouflage up and stuffed it in his pocket. It was one thing to have his mom laugh at it. He wanted to make sure all the kinks were worked out before he showed it to his dad.

"You can practice on me anytime," said Mr. Foote.

"Thanks, but you're kind of boring," said Owen. "Nothing personal."

He could hear his dad laughing as he headed back toward the house. He wanted to tighten the elastic on his headgear before he showed it to Joseph. And he needed to jot down a few observations about the spy business.

Like how important it was to pick the right person to spy on. And what a spy should do if the person was really boring. Maybe he could invent some way for him and Joseph to talk to each other without actually speaking. Some kind of Morse code.

Owen stopped. Morse code. It was perfect. He had a book in his room about Samuel Morse, the man who invented the Morse code. There was a list of the dots and dashes assigned to each letter of the alphabet in the back.

But how could they communicate in dots and dashes without making any noise? He made his way across the yard, deep in thought.

And then it came to him.

They could blink. That would do it.

Owen blinked his left eye experimentally. One blink of the left eye for "a," one blink of the right eye for "b."

Then maybe two blinks of the left eye for "c." Owen blinked his way hurriedly into the house. When he tripped on the lower step trying to blink both eyes for "e," he made a mental note.

Spies could blink, or they could walk. They shouldn't try to blink and walk at the same time.

2

The Ultimate Spy Test

"What did you just say?"

"I said, 'How are you?'"

"Oh." Owen frowned. "Why would a spy want to ask another spy how they were?"

"I don't know," said Joseph. "I couldn't think of anything else to say."

"Oh," said Owen again. He thought for a minute. "Maybe we shouldn't have dots and dashes for every letter," he said finally. "Maybe we should have them for whole sentences."

"That might be better," Joseph said. He rubbed his eyes. "My eyelids were getting kind of tired."

Owen looked at the list of international Morse code symbols he'd copied from his book. "This is worthless," he said decisively. He took two new

pieces of paper from his drawer. "Let's both make a list, so we can practice at home in the mirror and stuff."

He handed a piece to Joseph. "Now. What do we need to say to one another when we're spying?"

"How about 'Let's get out of here,'" said Joseph.

"Okay. One blink of the left eye means 'Let's get out of here.'" Owen and Joseph both wrote it down. ". . . And one blink of the right eye means 'Stop making so much noise.'"

They scribbled some more.

"And how about two dots and a dash of the left eye for 'Get off my foot,'" said Owen, picking up speed. ". . . And two dots and a dash of the *right* eye for 'I think someone's coming.'"

Joseph wrote feverishly to keep up with him.

When Owen stopped, they inspected the series of dots and dashes on their papers.

"What about 'I have to go to the bathroom'?" said Joseph. He saw Owen's face. "I can't help it. Sometimes I do."

"I know, I know." Owen thought for a minute. "How about both eyes blinking once at the same time?"

"Yeah, and lots of jiggling up and down."

They laughed.

"Wait a minute. We left out 'yes' and 'no,'" said Owen. "We should have done the simple ones first. Come on." He stood up and put his list in his pocket. "I told Anthony we'd be at his uncle's house by four o'clock. We'll have to work this out as we go along."

Joseph jumped up and followed him down the stairs.

"We're going to the Gallos'," Owen yelled.

"Be home by five," came his mom's voice from the living room.

"I just thought of something," Joseph said when they got out on the road. "When you say 'left eye,' do you mean the person's left eye who's *blinking,* or the eye that's on the left when you're *looking* at them?"

"The left eye of the person who's blinking," said Owen.

"So it's the right eye to the person who's looking at them."

"Right."

"That could get kind of confusing," Joseph said doubtfully. "You know Anthony. He had to wear a red rubber band around his left hand to remind him which one it was until last year."

"We have to practice, that's all." Owen turned into Weathering Heights. It was a new neighborhood, filled with huge houses in tiny yards. The house Anthony's uncle was building was at the end of the road. "It wouldn't be much fun spying around here," said Owen, looking around. "All you'd have to do is look out your window."

"Yeah. And even if you were just looking at some birds, everyone would think you were spying on them."

"If that was my bedroom," Owen said, pointing to a window in the side of a white house they were passing, "and that was yours," he pointed to a window in the house across a narrow strip of land from it, "we could use our Morse code."

"Cool," said Joseph. "At night, we could use flashlights."

"Yeah, and the real Morse code."

"Hey, you guys! Over here!" A hoarse whisper came from behind a house with a FOR SALE sign in front of it. It was Anthony. He beckoned to them madly.

"My uncle's house is the next one over," he said excitedly when they crouched down next to him. "There's a Dumpster in the back yard we can hide behind."

He was in camouflage from his head to his feet. He had on a camouflage hat, camouflage vest, camouflage pants—even his boots were camouflage. Professional camouflage, like you'd buy in a hunting store. His canteen was dappled green and brown, too. So were the binoculars he held up for them to see.

"My mom and dad got me these for scoring the most goals on my hockey team," he said. "They're really powerful. Want to try them?"

"Let's just get going," said Owen. "I have to be home in half an hour."

"Okay. Follow me." Anthony started to creep along the back of the house.

"Aren't you going to wear your camouflage?" Joseph asked Owen as they followed Anthony. Owen had put it in his pocket before they left the house.

"Are you joking?" Owen said it loud enough for Anthony to hear. "It's ridiculous to wear camouflage around here. There aren't any trees."

It really bugged him that Anthony always had the best equipment. Anthony acted like that was all it took to be good at something. But spying wasn't about equipment. It was about bravery and cunning.

It was about using your head in a pinch.

They reached the corner of the house. The Dumpster was straight ahead, about thirty feet away. They could hear loud hammering coming from inside the house. A table saw's shrill voice cried out from the garage. Somewhere, a radio was playing.

The familiar surge of excitement Owen always felt when he was about to zero in on his target erased any thoughts of being angry.

There was nothing between them and the Dumpster, overflowing with Sheetrock and scraps of lumber, except open space. Lots of open space. If anyone came out of the house before they reached cover, they were goners.

"Now!" he hissed.

He lit out for the Dumpster. Anthony and Joseph were right behind him. They dove in behind it like baseball players sliding into second base. They fell against it, breathless.

Owen rested his head against the Dumpster and waited for his heart to stop racing.

"That was a close one," said Anthony.

"Yeah," said Joseph. The three of them grinned at one another.

They heard a man's voice inside the house, and then someone laughed. But no one came out. They sat there for a while, listening. Anthony took out his binoculars and started fiddling with the lenses. The radio changed from music to the news.

Owen pulled his list out of his pocket.

"We came up with a special code," he said. "Maybe we should practice it while we wait."

Anthony gave it a quick glance. "How do you say, 'This is boring'?" he said. "All we're spying on is a house."

"Okay, okay." Owen stuffed his list back into his pocket. "Let's get closer."

"Closer?" said Joseph. "I kind of like it here."

"You can stay, then," said Anthony. He was already on his feet. "I say let's go look in a window."

"A window?" Joseph's voice was a yelp. "What window?"

"Anthony's right," said Owen. "It's not really spying if we don't see anybody." He pulled Joseph to his feet. "We'll run up, look in a window, and leave. It'll be fine."

"That window there," said Anthony. He pointed to a picture window next to the front door. "You guys ready?"

"Ready," said Owen.

"Not ready," said Joseph.

"Go!"

They dashed out from behind the Dumpster

and headed for the window. Owen reached it first. He looked inside.

A worker was standing with his back to them. He was so close Owen could have reached out and touched him. Owen ducked down. He motioned for Anthony and Joseph to do the same.

But it was too late.

"Hey, you kids!" shouted a deep voice above their heads. "Get out of here!"

It was hard to tell who shrieked the loudest. Owen was halfway across the yard with Anthony and Joseph on his heels. He could hear their feet pounding the pavement as they raced down the street.

He didn't stop running until he reached the entrance to Weathering Heights. Then he threw himself on the ground, exhausted. Anthony and Joseph fell in a heap next to him.

It was a few minutes before any of them could talk.

"Did you see how big that guy was?" Anthony said at last.

"I thought he was coming after us." Joseph's face was bright red.

"I thought I was going to have a heart attack when he yelled like that," Anthony said.

"I couldn't believe it!" said Owen. "I could have tapped him on the shoulder, he was so close!"

He sat up. The thing about spying was, the more terrified you were while you were doing it, the greater you felt when it was over. "That was so cool," he said.

"Yeah." Anthony and Joseph looked at him and grinned.

They slapped palms. "I better get going," Owen said. He stood up. "I have to be home by five."

"I've got to go, too," said Anthony. His house was in the opposite direction. "Let's spy on someone in the woods next time, so I can use my gear. See ya."

"That was a lot more exciting than spying on my parents," Joseph said as he and Owen walked along. His face was still red, but he sounded happy. "I never knew I could run that fast."

"It's like my dad says," said Owen. "You never know what you can do until you have to." He was thinking about what they'd done, what they should have done differently. "Next time, we have to remember to use our code. We didn't use it at all."

"I guess when someone yells at you about two inches from your head, you don't really need to say, 'Let's get out of here,'" said Joseph. "At least, not in words."

"You can say that again," said Owen.

"I can see me now. I would have been standing there like an idiot, blinking my head off, with you and Anthony halfway down the street."

Owen laughed. "Yeah. This huge guy is looming over you," he raised his arms in the air and moved toward Joseph like a monster, "and you're going blink-blink. Blink, blink, blink."

"What's wrong, kid?" Joseph said in a deep voice. "Got something in your eye?"

They cracked each other up until Joseph turned down his street. It was amazing how funny everything seemed when you'd just escaped incredible danger.

* * *

"How did your camouflage work?" said Lydia. She had stopped in the door to Owen's room on her way back from her shower.

"I didn't use it." Owen kept his head down and wrote carefully. Mr. Foote had said he would make copies of their code at work tomorrow. Owen had been trying since dinner to come up with more things to add.

"Why not? I'm sure the workers could have used a good laugh."

"There weren't any trees." Owen finished copying the last symbol and looked up. "Anthony had on professional camouflage from his head to his feet. I bet his underwear was camouflage."

"Wait till you get to middle school." Lydia came into his room and perched on the end of his bed. "There are tons of kids like Anthony. Everyone has designer labels on their clothing, their shoes, their hats, their watches . . ."

"Maybe I'll skip middle school," said Owen. "Anthony drives me crazy."

"Remember Amanda Fuller? The one I went to camp with in fifth grade? She was like that." Lydia took the towel hanging around her neck and rubbed her wet hair. "You're lucky. Boys just brag about their stuff. Girls cut you out of their group if you don't have the right things."

"You probably don't want to be part of their group, anyway, do you?"

"No. But you don't want them to make the decision for you."

"Anthony's parents give him money for good grades," said Owen. "He has his own computer and his own VCR. They just gave him a pair of binoculars for scoring the most goals in hockey." It felt good to be able to talk to Lydia about Anthony. She didn't lecture him like his mom would have.

"His parents are jerks," said Lydia. "I remember his father standing on the sidelines, *screaming* at the poor kid, when you guys played soccer in kindergarten. Kindergarten, for pete's sake. And all his mother does is work."

"It would be nice to get five dollars for A's, though, wouldn't it?" Owen said. "You and I would clean up."

"Maybe. But then you never would have invented your underwear mask. Or any of your other crazy inventions," she said, standing up. "You'd be as boring as Anthony."

"If you really like it, I could make you one," said Owen. "I'd sell it to you for five dollars."

"Dream on, Owen," Lydia said. She headed down the hall toward her room.

"Two dollars!" Owen shouted.

Lydia's door closed.

Darn! He could have used that money to buy some wire for the human battery experiment he wanted to try. Just in case the Morse code didn't catch on.

Owen took his spy journal off his desk and flopped down on his bed. Lydia thought Anthony was boring. Owen could tell she thought he, Owen, was interesting, even though she didn't say so. She liked his inventions, too.

He tapped his pencil against the page. Spying on the Gallos' house had been kind of boring until that man yelled at them. Then it became terrifying.

Therefore, the scarier the person they spied on, the more exciting it would be. Who did they know who would be really scary?

Later that night, the answer woke him up out of a sound sleep. Owen sat straight up in his bed and stared into the dark as if he had seen a ghost.

Mr. Mahoney. The principal of Chesterfield School.

Just *thinking* about spying on Mr. Mahoney sent a shiver down his spine.

Mr. Mahoney was awesome. He used to be in the Marines. He still was, one weekend a month. From the muscles in his chest and arms, Owen bet he lifted weights on the other weekends.

Owen liked Mr. Mahoney a lot. Most of the kids did. But they were scared of him, too.

He lay slowly back down and pulled the covers up to his chin.

Spying on Mr. Mahoney would be the ultimate spy test. The one that separated the spies with nerves of steel from all the rest.

He could hardly wait to tell Joseph and Anthony about it tomorrow. He could hardly wait to see their faces.

3

What Does Underwear Have to Do with Camouflage?

"Mr. Mahoney?" said Anthony. "Are you crazy?"

"Shhh." Owen put his finger to his lips and looked back over his shoulder. "Not so loud."

Anthony leaned toward him across the cafeteria table. "You're nuts, Owen," he whispered.

"I don't know." Joseph's eyes were enormous. "I don't think Mr. Mahoney would like kids spying on him."

"That's the whole point, Joseph. I realized it after the Gallos' house yesterday," Owen said. He pried open his carton of milk. "We're too experienced to keep on spying on *normal* people. We've got to raise the stakes. Add a little danger." He paused. "Mr. Mahoney would be the *ultimate spy test.*"

Owen leaned heavily on each word, watching them. He wished he had x-ray eyes. He would have loved to watch his words sinking into their brains. Sending off a tiny burst of flame as each one hit home.

But he didn't need x-ray eyes. Their faces told him they knew he was right.

"There's no telling what we might see him doing," he said enticingly. "Crushing stones, doing about a million push-ups." He took a swig of milk. "We might even see him scaling the side of his house. I bet he does, to stay in shape."

"His *house?*" Anthony's mouth fell open. Owen could see pale yellow lumps of egg salad. "You mean, not at school?"

"What's there to see at school?" said Owen. "All he does is walk around the halls."

"But on his own personal property?" Joseph asked. For once, Joseph was siding with Anthony, not him. "Spying's one thing, Owen. Trespassing's another."

"What do you think real spies do?" said Owen.

"Sneak around their own property, watching their own family all the time?"

"That's what *I* do," said Anthony.

"Me, too," said Joseph.

"I do, too," said Owen impatiently. "But it's getting boring. My parents don't do anything, and all Lydia does is talk on the phone or read. And what about yesterday? Yesterday was boring until that guy yelled at us."

He leaned forward so he could talk in a lower voice. "We wouldn't have to go on the Mahoneys' property, Joseph. My dad goes jogging on the paths in the woods behind their house all the time. The woods belong to the town. They aren't private property."

"What's not private property?" Ben Carter tossed his lunch bag on the table next to Joseph and sat down. "What are you guys talking about?"

"Nothing." Owen quickly picked up his sandwich and took a bite. He shot Joseph and Anthony a warning look. "Right, guys?"

"Right," said Joseph.

But Anthony couldn't stop himself. He was jiggling around in his seat like a Mexican jumping bean, he was so excited. "We're going to spy on Mr. Mahoney," he said in a loud whisper. "At his *house.*"

"Cool." Ben looked impressed. "Can I come?"

"Owen's kind of in charge," Joseph said. "It was his idea."

Ben turned to him. "Can I?"

"I don't know," Owen said slowly. He took another bite of his sandwich to stall for time. He wasn't sure about Ben. Ben had been in Owen's class since the first grade, but he wasn't really Owen's friend.

Not the way Joseph was. Or even Anthony.

Ben used to make fun of Owen because he was small for his age. But then Owen stood up for him in front of the school nurse on height and weight chart day.

Ben never gave him a hard time again.

Still, Owen wasn't sure he could trust Ben. He was always bragging about something. Either about how strong he was or about how cool his two older brothers were. About the wild things they did. The trouble they got into.

Letting a kid like Ben in on their plans made Owen uneasy.

He swallowed his sandwich and took another swig of his milk. "It takes a lot of practice to be a spy," he said finally. "Joseph and Anthony and me have a lot of experience."

"I do, too," said Ben. "My brothers taught me how to spy when I was about two. We spy on this old lady who lives next door all the time. Come on, you guys. I can bring my brothers' walkie-talkies."

"Walkie-talkies?" Anthony's eyes lit up. "My parents said that if do a good job on the end-of-grade test, they'll buy me a set. They're so cool. Come on, Owen. Let him come."

He should have known Anthony would go for the walkie-talkies, Owen thought with disgust. He looked at Joseph. He didn't need Morse code to know that Joseph felt the same way he did.

But they both knew it was too late to keep Ben out.

"It might be fun," Joseph said to him hopefully. "We could be in teams. You and me, and Anthony and Ben. We could have one walkie-talkie and they could have the other one."

"Okay," Owen said. "You can come. But you can't tell anyone else. No one can. If anyone blabs, they're out."

He held up his hand with the pinkie stuck out. "Deal?"

Joseph, Anthony, and Ben locked their pinkies over his.

"Deal," they said solemnly.

"This Saturday?"

"This Saturday."

A feeling of excitement ran through them like an electric current. Then a heavy hand clamped down on Owen's shoulder.

A familiar voice said, "You boys look very serious."

Joseph looked as if he'd been caught with his hand on the lock to a Wells Fargo truck. Anthony jerked back in his chair as if someone had shoved him. Ben stopped chewing. He lowered his sandwich to the table with his eyes glued to the space above Owen's head.

Owen turned around. "Hi, Mr. Mahoney."

"If I didn't know better, I'd think you were planning a dangerous military mission," said Mr. Mahoney. He looked around the group with a friendly smile. "What are you boys up to?"

His hand felt like a steel clamp on Owen's shoulder. One firm squeeze and Owen's bones would crumble like pretzels.

"Not much," Ben said.

"We were just talking." Owen's face felt hot.

"Talking about some pretty serious stuff, I'd say," said Mr. Mahoney. He patted Owen's shoulder. "I'm looking for Mrs. Furlone. Have any of you seen her?"

"She's over there with Mr. Hall's class," said Ben. He pointed to the back of the cafeteria. "Someone spilled their milk on the table."

"So she is," said Mr. Mahoney. "Thank you, Ben." He patted Owen's shoulder again. "I'd better see if she needs help. See you boys later."

One last squeeze and he was gone.

Owen sagged against the back of his chair. "That was a close one," he said.

"You were great." Joseph was looking at him with huge eyes. "You didn't sound nervous at all."

"It's a good thing you guys did the talking," said Anthony. "I think my voice box was paralyzed."

"Do you think he heard anything?" Owen looked around the group.

"Nah. No one can hear anything in the cafeteria," said Ben.

"I guess you're right," said Owen. He craned his head around to see where Mr. Mahoney was. When Mrs. Furlone, the cafeteria monitor, slapped the end of their table with her hand, he almost fell out of his chair.

"Line up, boys," she said. "You've left some chips under the table, Anthony. Ben, I believe that's your napkin." She looked at Joseph. "Joseph? Are you okay? You look a little pale."

"I'm fine."

"Okay. Whose turn is it to clean up?"

"Anthony's and mine," said Ben.

"Then you'd better hurry," said Mrs. Furlone. "Everyone else is already in line."

Ben and Anthony rushed to get a wet cloth for

the table and a broom. Owen and Joseph went to throw away their trash.

"What if we get caught?" said Joseph. His face was back to its usual color, but his eyes looked worried. "He almost caught us then and we weren't even spying."

"We're not going to get caught," Owen said firmly. "I'll make you some camouflage like mine. He won't be able to see us. I promise."

"My dad doesn't wear the kind that look like shorts," said Joseph. He got in line behind Owen. "He wears the kind with the 'y' in front. I'll look like I'm wearing a shower cap."

"Don't worry," Owen said. "My dad probably has another pair. You can come over tomorrow after school to see if they fit. We can practice our Morse code, too."

* * *

"*Another* pair?" said Mrs. Foote. "Your father's going to think I'm burying his boxer shorts in the same underwear cemetery where I bury his socks."

"These were in the garage. Dad was going to

use them as a rag." Owen smoothed out the pair of boxer shorts on the coffee table. They had a large hole in the back. "I have to make a pair for Joseph. He's a nervous wreck he'll get caught."

Owen bit his lip, but it was too late.

"Caught?" said his mom. She looked alert, as if Owen had just sent up a flare. "Who are you spying on, that he's worried about getting caught? Do you think maybe you're getting a little carried away with all this spying, Owen?"

It was his dad who came to his rescue.

"If he is, it's genetic," he said, stooping to kiss his wife on the cheek. He put his briefcase on the couch. "His mother is a voyeur at heart."

"I know what that means," said Lydia. She looked up from her homework. Ever since she had started taking French in middle school, she acted as if she'd been born in France. "It means . . ." She frowned. "I forget."

"It means Mom's a spy," said Owen. "Like me."

"I am *not*," said his mom. "I like to see how other people live, that's all. I should have been an anthropologist."

"Do anthropologists give fake names to realtors at model homes?" said Owen.

"And do they drive around at night, hoping people have left their curtains open so they can see into their living room windows?" said Lydia.

Mr. Foote laughed. "Looks like they've got your number, honey."

"It's not spying," insisted Mrs. Foote. "I find it interesting, that's all. It's like looking at a play, or a painting."

"Face it, Mom. You're a spy," said Owen. He stood up. "You can sneak over to the Gallos' house with me sometime. You'll love it. Their garage is bigger than our whole house."

"She's getting interested," teased Mr. Foote. "I see that gleam in her eye."

"I do not sneak," said Mrs. Foote primly. She swatted Mr. Foote with the newspaper. "Whose side are you on, anyway?"

"The right side," said Owen. He started for the door.

"Where are you going?" said his mom. "It's your night to set the table."

"Not yet. I've got to get started on Joseph's camouflage."

"What's wrong?" said Lydia. "Doesn't Mr. Hobbs wear the right kind of underwear?"

"The right kind of underwear?" Mr. Foote looked from her to Owen. "What does Mr. Hobbs's underwear have to do with camouflage?"

"You don't want to know, Dad," Lydia said.

"Don't tell him," said Owen. "I want him to be surprised."

"Oh, he'll be surprised, all right," said Lydia. "It's whether he'll finally have you committed that I'm wondering about."

4

Fancy Meeting You Here

"Come in, Owen. Come in, Owen."

Owen held the walkie-talkie up to his mouth and pressed the button. "Owen here."

"Green car alert. Green car alert." Anthony's voice was full of static.

"Over and out," said Owen. He clicked off the walkie-talkie, shouted, "Duck or die!" and hurled himself into the ditch by the side of the road.

Joseph dove behind a pile of rocks.

They were just in time. A green car came flying around the corner and sped past them in a blast of warm air.

"Whew! That was a close one." Joseph crawled out from behind his hiding spot. "That guy was going fast."

The car had disappeared around the corner.

"You know whose road is down there, don't you?" said Owen.

The smile slid from Joseph's face.

"I'd better call them in." Owen pushed the speak button. "Owen to Anthony. Owen to Anthony."

There was a squawk, then a voice. "What's up?"

It was Ben.

"Enemy territory straight ahead," said Owen. "We'll wait for you. Over and out." He put the walkie-talkie in his back pocket and looked at Joseph.

The game was over.

Owen had invented it the night before while he was lying in bed, thinking about Ben's walkie-talkies. He named it "Duck or Die." The way it worked was that he and Joseph were one team, Anthony and Ben were the other, and cars were the enemy.

He and Joseph had started down the road first. Anthony and Ben gave them a five-minute lead. Then they started walking, too.

If a car came from their direction, Anthony and Ben had to radio a warning to Owen and Joseph. If it came from *their* direction, Owen and Joseph had to warn them.

If a car got to your team before you hid, you were dead.

It was a lot of fun. They had been playing it for more than an hour now. They had worked their way down Chesterfield Road, jumping over bushes and rolling on the ground.

But now Mr. Mahoney's road was around the corner. The real game was about to begin.

Anthony and Ben ran up to them. They were out of breath.

"Mr. Mahoney's road is right down there," said Owen. They looked to where he was pointing and nodded solemnly. "We can cut through the woods here and get there in about five minutes. No more talking. And no more walkie-talkies."

"No fair," said Anthony. "They're the best part."

"Owen's right," Ben said. He put his in his pocket. "They make too much noise."

"You know Mr. Mahoney," Joseph said nervously. "He hears everything. Even things kids haven't said yet."

They all looked at one another. It was true.

Some kids at school said Mr. Mahoney had a radio receiver implanted in his ear. Other kids swore he could read minds.

No one felt safe having bad thoughts when Mr. Mahoney was around. Much less doing bad things.

And here they were, getting ready to spy on him in his own back yard.

Joseph coughed. Owen knew what that meant. If they didn't go right now, Joseph might either change his mind or throw up. If he threw up, they'd *all* change their minds.

Owen pulled his camouflage down over his head. "Come on," he said gruffly.

He jumped over the ditch and started into the woods. Joseph and Anthony and Ben scrambled up the small hill behind him. No one wanted to be left behind.

Owen walked as quietly as he could. The other boys followed behind him, single file. Owen held on to branches that stuck out in front of him so they wouldn't whip back and hit anyone in the face.

For a few minutes they walked in silence. There was no one else around.

Then Owen spotted something through the trees. He stopped and motioned toward it. When everyone had seen it, he started moving again, cautiously.

It was a house. A brown house. Owen let the air seep slowly out of him with relief.

The Mahoneys' house was red. He wasn't ready to reach the Mahoneys' house. Not just yet.

They filed past the brown house silently. There was a trampoline on one side of the yard and a wooden swing set in the middle. Owen saw a fenced-in area with a small doghouse inside.

His heart stopped beating.

What if the Mahoneys had a dog? He hadn't thought of that. It would be a military dog, if they did, knowing Mr. Mahoney. Trained to sniff out spies at a hundred yards. To run them to the ground and stand over them—snarling—until the Marines arrived.

Owen wracked his mind, trying to remember.

A cool sweat broke out on his forehead. If he asked the other guys, they might get cold feet. Joseph would know why he was asking, for sure.

So he kept walking. After a few minutes, they passed a yellow house. That yard was deserted, too. It started to feel as if all they were doing was taking an innocent walk in the woods.

When he heard sounds of scuffling behind him, Owen turned around. Anthony was holding Ben's walkie-talkie up above his head. Ben was trying to shove him off balance.

"Quiet," Owen said in a low voice. "We're getting close."

Ben snatched the walkie-talkie out of Anthony's hand. They fell into line again.

Then Owen saw it through the trees.

The side of a dark red house. He pointed to it silently. The mood was suddenly tense.

Looking at the Mahoneys' house, he wondered if maybe they should go back to playing "Duck or Die" instead. Mess around with the walkie-talkies some more. Anthony would like that, he knew.

Then Joseph whispered in his ear, "Maybe this isn't such a good idea."

That did it. No way was he going to chicken out now. Owen kept walking, leading them along the ridge that ran along the rear of the Mahoneys' back yard. It wasn't high, but it was steep. A straight drop of dirt and rocks down to grass. The edge looked crumbly, so Owen kept away from it.

He was heading toward a clump of bushes halfway along the ridge. It would make the perfect spying place.

Down below, the Mahoneys' yard was empty. There was a deck with a round table and chairs. A book was lying open on a table next to a blue-striped chaise longue.

Owen saw a barbecue grill next to the deck, and a garden in the middle of the yard. There was a shovel sticking out of it, as if whoever had been working had suddenly been called away.

Maybe the Mahoneys weren't even at home, Owen thought suddenly. Maybe they had gone grocery shopping. The possibility made him giddy with relief.

Then a door slammed and he froze.

Mrs. Mahoney came out onto the deck carrying a tall glass. She put the glass on the table next to the book. She sat down on the end of the chaise and untied her sneakers.

She dropped them on the deck, swung her legs onto the cushion, and picked up the book.

She started to read.

Owen was afraid to breathe.

If they moved, Mrs. Mahoney might look up and see them. If they stayed here—frozen in plain sight—she'd *definitely* see them.

He headed for the bushes as fast as he could without running. When he slid in behind them, Joseph, Anthony, and Ben were fast on his heels. The clump wasn't nearly as big as it had looked.

They had to scrunch up into little balls and wrap their arms around their knees so no one's arm or leg would stick out.

They were jockeying noiselessly for position when the door slammed again. Owen looked down.

It was Mr. Mahoney.

He handed his wife a bowl and said something that made her laugh. Then he walked down the steps and over to the garden. He grabbed the shovel and started to dig.

Owen turned his head and saw Anthony and Joseph and Ben staring at him like deer caught in the headlights of a car.

They were actually doing it. They were spying on Mr. Mahoney.

Up till now, spying on Mr. Mahoney had been an *idea*. Owen had never really gotten so far as to imagine how it would feel to finally *see* Mr. Mahoney.

Now he knew. It would feel terrifying.

Here was Mr. Mahoney, the principal of Chesterfield School, relaxing in his own back yard. And here was Owen, crammed behind a bush with three other kids, spying on him.

If they moved, Mr. Mahoney would hear them.

If they ran, Mr. Mahoney would see them.

The bush seemed to be growing smaller by the second.

Mr. Mahoney was working his way slowly down a garden row, turning over the soil one methodical shovelful at a time. Every once in a while, he or Mrs. Mahoney said something. But mostly, they were quiet.

For a few minutes, no one behind the bush moved. They kept their eyes trained on Mr. Mahoney. Then gradually, the shock began to wear off. Owen could think. And what he thought was that Mr. Mahoney looked amazingly normal.

He was hypnotized by his garden the same way Owen's dad was. He was wearing a hat with a brim that went all the way around it, like the one Owen's dad wore.

And it looked just as corny.

Even the dark stain spreading over the middle of his back looked like plain old sweat. Mr. Mahoney looked like a happy man enjoying his privacy in his own back yard.

Watching him, Owen came to a terrible realization. He would *hate* it if Mr. Mahoney did anything embarrassing. He didn't want to be able to laugh about him afterward with Joseph and Anthony and Ben. He didn't want Mr. Mahoney to do anything that would make him look silly.

He wanted Mr. Mahoney to be Mr. Mahoney, awesome principal of Chesterfield School.

He felt someone squirming beside him. Ben made a face and pointed to his legs. Owen knew what he meant. His legs were starting to ache, too. And his camouflage was itching like crazy.

He took it off and looked over at the other guys. Joseph still looked worried, but Anthony made a face. A "This is boring" face.

Owen looked at his watch. They had only been here for fifteen minutes. It felt more like fifteen hours. Mr. Mahoney got to the end of the row and started on another.

Owen counted. There were ten rows in all. Nine more left. Nine times fifteen. Owen didn't even have to do the math. This was going to go on for a long time.

Someone tapped him on the shoulder.

It was Anthony. He jerked his thumb back over his shoulder. Owen shook his head. There was no way they could move without Mr. Mahoney hearing them.

Next to him, Joseph was trying to get comfortable. He rocked back and forth on his bottom. Owen had to put a hand on the ground to keep from being knocked over.

There was nothing they could do but wait.

Joseph nudged him with his elbow and blinked. "What?" Owen mouthed.

Joseph blinked again. Owen shook his head to say he didn't understand. "The *bathroom*," Joseph whispered.

Anthony clamped his hand over his mouth and started to move his shoulders up and down, as if he was laughing.

Owen glared at him to make him stop, but it was no use. Anthony wasn't afraid anymore. He was bored. So was Ben. He leaned against Joseph and made a soft hissing sound. "Psssss."

Anthony started to laugh for real. Ben did, too. They were jiggling around, banging against one another, like twin volcanoes about to erupt. There wasn't enough room in that small space to contain them.

Before Owen knew what was happening, they bumped into Joseph, Joseph bumped into him, and he was sent sprawling out from behind the bush.

And then he was falling. Tumbling head over heels down the hill with dirt flying up around his face and rocks jabbing into his back. His camouflage was ripped out of his hands. He grabbed a branch and felt prickers dig into his skin.

It was over as quickly as it had begun.

Owen landed on his back at the bottom of the hill so hard it knocked the wind out of him. He lay there in a daze and heard the sound of the other boys crashing away through the woods above him.

Then he heard an even worse sound.

Footsteps.

Mr. Mahoney's face blotted out the blue sky above Owen's head like a storm cloud.

"Owen Foote," he said pleasantly. "Fancy meeting you here."

5

"Punish Us Now. Please."

"Who is it? Is he all right?" Mrs. Mahoney came running across the yard.

"It's Owen Foote, and he's fine," said Mr. Mahoney. He helped Owen to his feet. "He's a little scratched up, that's all."

Mrs. Mahoney's worried face peered into Owen's. "We always warned our sons to be careful on that ridge," she said. "No matter how many bushes we plant, it keeps eroding. What were you *doing* up there?"

Mr. Mahoney didn't have to ask. When he came back down the hill, he had Owen's camouflage in his hand.

"Nice job," he said, holding it out. "You made it yourself?"

All Owen could do was nod.

Mrs. Mahoney was making worried noises, checking him over for damage.

"Oh, dear," she said. She took Owen's left hand in her own. "Your hand's bleeding."

"It doesn't hurt," Owen lied. He pulled it away and rubbed it against his pants.

Mr. Mahoney patted his wife on the shoulder. "He's fine, Patsy. I can take it from here."

He sounded the way he did in school when there was a problem. It meant he was in charge, and everyone should leave. It always worked. People melted away fast. No one wanted to be around when the trouble started.

"All right, dear." Mrs. Mahoney gave Owen a quick smile. "If you want a Band-Aid for that, you let me know."

She left.

Mr. Mahoney looked up at the top of the ridge. "It appears your troops have deserted you," he said.

Owen looked up, too. Mr. Mahoney must have heard them running away. Now he was waiting for Owen to give him an explanation. Owen looked down at the ground.

He couldn't think of a thing to say. He was as empty as the ridge.

Then he heard a cough.

Owen looked up and saw Joseph walking carefully toward the edge of the ridge. His face was bright red. The camouflage flap on his hat was dangling over one shoulder by a thread.

To Owen, he had never looked more wonderful.

"I thought you might not be far away, Joseph," said Mr. Mahoney. "Be careful coming down."

Joseph partly slid, partly stumbled his way down the hill. When he got to the bottom, Mr. Mahoney grabbed him by the arm to keep him from falling.

Joseph darted a nervous glance at Owen.

"So," said Mr. Mahoney. He stood there smiling at them, waiting. He didn't say another word.

He didn't have to. A whole silent conversation was going on among the three of them. Owen and Joseph knew that Mr. Mahoney knew that they had been spying. And Mr. Mahoney knew that they knew he knew.

Now he was waiting to see what they would say.

Owen's brain was careening around like a car on an obstacle course. He couldn't tell the truth— it was too embarrassing. But he couldn't lie, either. Mr. Mahoney was an expert in kids lying. He told them the same thing every year at the School Spirit assembly.

Owen had heard it three times now.

"You should always tell the truth because you know it's the right thing to do," he'd say. "But in case you ever get confused about what's the truth and what's not, I have my own lie detector right up here."

Then he'd tap his forehead slowly—three times—while he looked around the crowded bleachers. "It can spot a lie a mile away."

Every kid in the gym felt like Mr. Mahoney's eyes were boring right into their brain. Their brain, stuffed with possible lies and mean thoughts. They'd all stare back at him in awe.

The way Owen and Joseph were doing right now.

It was Joseph who finally spoke. "What are you going to do?" he said.

"Do?" Mr. Mahoney rubbed his stubbly chin. "That's a good question, Joseph. I guess what I do will depend on what you tell me *you* were doing."

It was going from bad to worse.

"I'll tell you what," said Mr. Mahoney suddenly. "Let's not talk about this right now. Let's all think about it for a week. You two come back next Saturday and we'll talk about it then. Okay?"

No, not okay, Owen wanted to say. Punish us now and get it over with.

Please.

But Mr. Mahoney was already leading them across the yard toward the road. He was saying something friendly about his garden. As if Owen and Joseph had stopped by to buy tomatoes or something.

Owen and Joseph stumbled along beside him like sleepwalkers in the middle of a nightmare.

Mr. Mahoney stopped when they got to the corner of the garage. "You might want to put something on that hand when you get home," he said to Owen. "I've got to get back to work, boys. I'll see you in school."

"Okay." Owen raised his hand in the air, then let it drop back to his side. "Bye."

"Yeah," said Joseph. "Bye."

They had almost made it to the road when Mr. Mahoney called out to them. "Oh, and Owen," he said in a loud voice.

Owen and Joseph both turned around.

"If any of the other troops want to come with you, they're welcome."

"Oh. Thanks," said Owen. He started to walk again. All he wanted to do was get away. To get off this road and away from this house as fast as possible.

He didn't say a word to Joseph. He didn't even look at him. He wouldn't blame Joseph if he hated him for the rest of his life.

Then Joseph said, "Sorry I ran away, Owen."

Owen looked at him. "*You're* sorry?" he said. "What do you mean? *I* got us into this mess."

Joseph shrugged. "Yeah, but before it was a mess, it was exciting."

"I thought I was going to throw up when I saw Mr. Mahoney's face," Owen said.

"I did, too," said Joseph, "when I knocked you down the hill."

"You didn't knock me. Ben and Anthony did."

"They couldn't help it. There was no room."

They started to walk again. Joseph was right. Owen couldn't blame anyone. They had made a plan, and it had failed.

What mattered now was next Saturday.

"Where did Anthony and Ben go?" he said.

"I don't know." Joseph shrugged. "Home, probably."

More silence. "You know, that's the first time I've ever been to Mr. Mahoney's office," Joseph said finally. "Well, not his office. You know what I mean."

"It's not as scary when you're at school. He expects you to be bad there."

"Yeah. I don't think he was expecting you to roll down the hill like that."

"Probably not," said Owen. "What did he look like?"

"A little surprised."

"I bet." Owen kicked halfheartedly at a stone in the road. "I wish it was Sunday," he said finally. "I mean, next Sunday."

"Me, too," Joseph said.

And then they didn't say any more. Because there was nothing more to say.

* * *

Ben and Anthony were waiting for them at the corner of Chesterfield Road. "What did he do? What did he say?" Anthony was hopping up and down, waiting to hear the worst. "Was he mad? I bet he was furious."

Owen looked at Ben. Ben's hands were hanging down at his sides. His face had a look on it Owen couldn't read.

"What's your punishment?" Anthony said eagerly. "What's he going to do—give you a thousand weeks of detention?"

He said it like it was funny. Like the whole thing had been a spy movie, and not real life. And that Owen and Joseph were just actors who had gotten caught.

Not friends Anthony had deserted.

"Where'd you guys go?" Owen said. He was suddenly very angry. "Why'd you run away like that? You should have come back, like Joseph."

"Are you crazy?" said Anthony. "No way I was going to hang around and get in trouble. We were out of there. Right, Ben?"

"I ran." Ben's voice was flat. "I didn't even think about it. I just ran."

Owen was suddenly sick of the whole thing. "Yeah, well, thanks a lot, you guys," he said disgustedly. "Let's go, Joseph."

He and Joseph started to walk again.

"Come on, Owen, tell us what he said," said Anthony.

"He said we have to go back there next Saturday," Owen said over his shoulder. "He said the rest of our troops should come with us."

That wasn't entirely true, he knew. Mr. Mahoney had said they *could* come back, not should. Owen didn't think Mr. Mahoney even knew who the other kids were. But why should he tell them that?

Let them stew.

Anthony ran to catch up to them. "You didn't

tell him who was with you, did you?" He looked from Owen to Joseph and back to Owen again. "Did you?"

"That's for us to know and you to find out. Right, Joseph?"

"Right."

"No fair. Come on, you guys," Anthony wheedled. "You didn't, did you?" He stopped, but Owen and Joseph kept walking.

"Did you?" he yelled.

"Maybe. Maybe not," shouted Owen. He threw his arm over Joseph's shoulder.

"We'll let them sweat it out," he said.

"Yeah," said Joseph. "Like we're going to."

It wasn't a huge consolation, but it was better than nothing.

6

Taking It Like a Man

"It's going to be a long week," said Mr. Foote.

"A very long week," said Lydia. "With a terrible ending."

Mrs. Foote rested her hand on Lydia's arm. "I don't think Owen needs to hear that, Lydia."

Owen moved a piece of lettuce over to cover up his potato salad. The last thing he wanted right now was food. Now that he was home, now that he'd watched his parents' reaction, the heady feeling of being a comrade-in-arms with Joseph had disappeared.

He had told them what had happened, but not how he had felt. How he had felt was not something he wanted to say out loud.

The humiliation of lying there on the ground with Mr. Mahoney looking down at him. The shame of standing there with his mouth hanging open, with nothing to say. Of not having the guts to tell the truth. Those kinds of things were impossible to talk about.

When he got to the part about Joseph, Lydia thumped the table with her fist. "Good old Joseph!" she said.

"That was a brave thing for him to do," said Mr. Foote.

"I know," said Owen. "Mr. Mahoney knew there were others. He could hear them running away. But I didn't tell him who. He said they could come back with Joseph and me next Saturday."

"Will they?" said his mom.

"Anthony said he wouldn't."

"What about Ben?"

"I don't know." Owen shrugged. "Probably not."

"Mr. Mahoney, of all people," said Lydia. She shook her head in amazement. "That's a wacky idea, even for you, Owen."

"It certainly has gotten very complicated," said their dad. "But Owen can handle it."

"You don't think we could call?" His mom looked hopefully at his dad.

"No." Owen and his dad said it at the same time.

"Dad's right," Owen said. "Joseph and me can handle it."

Owen's mom didn't bother to correct his grammar.

"What do you think he'll do?" said Lydia.

"Mr. Mahoney is a very fair man," Mrs. Foote said firmly. "I'm sure it will be something reasonable."

Owen and Lydia looked at each other.

Maybe Mom's right, said Owen's face.

Not a chance, answered Lydia's.

* * *

Owen was almost glad when he woke up on Saturday morning. Between Anthony bugging him and his trying to avoid Mr. Mahoney in the halls, it had been the longest week of his life.

He didn't think he'd slept a wink all week. Every time he closed his eyes, visions of Saturday morning ran through his brain like a video.

He and Joseph would walk up to Mr. Mahoney's house. They'd knock on Mr. Mahoney's door. Mr. Mahoney would open it and say . . . Owen's eyes popped open every time.

He couldn't begin to imagine what Mr. Mahoney was going to say. Or do.

Standing at the front door with his mom, Owen felt like a prisoner taking his last lonely stroll.

"If you're not home in two days, we'll send out the police," Lydia called cheerfully from the study.

"Lydia, that's mean." Mrs. Foote looked at Owen with a worried face. "You look tired, sweetie. Are you sure you feel all right?"

"For Heaven's sake!" Lydia shouted. "He's practically going to jail! How do you expect him to look?"

Owen's mom came outside, closed the door behind them, and put her arm around his shoulders. "Are you sure you don't want me to drive you?"

"No, thanks." Owen put on his helmet and walked over to his bike. "Joseph's riding his bike, too. We want to be able to make a fast getaway."

"I'm sure everything will be fine," said his mom. "I'll have a nice lunch waiting when you get home."

"Okay," Owen said. "Bye." He kicked up his

kickstand and pushed off without looking back. He knew his mom was standing there, watching him.

When he turned onto Chesterfield Road, Joseph was riding toward him from the other direction.

They met halfway.

"Hi," Joseph said.

"Hi." They looked at each other for a minute. Then Owen shrugged. "I guess we'd better get going."

"Yeah. We don't want to add tardiness on top of everything else."

They rode in silence until they neared Mr. Mahoney's road. Someone was sitting on the grass on the corner.

It was Ben. He stood up when he saw them coming.

"What are you doing here?" said Owen, amazed.

"I'm coming with you," said Ben. He picked his bike up off the grass.

"Why?" said Joseph.

"I was there, wasn't I?"

"Yeah, but he doesn't know."

"We let you think he did, to punish you," said

Owen. "Well, not you so much. Anthony. Mr. Mahoney doesn't know anything."

"Well, I do." Ben jutted out his jaw. "What kind of chicken do you think I am?"

There was a heavy silence between them. Then Owen said, "Fried?"

Ben only snorted, but Owen could see he thought it was a good answer. They hopped on their bikes and started to ride.

Owen almost felt good as he pedaled. It was the three of them, side by side, in the middle of the road. The cavalry, riding to face the enemy.

His bubble burst when Mrs. Mahoney answered the door. "Mr. Mahoney's down in the basement, boys." She smiled at them encouragingly. "Go right down."

They filed past her with Owen in the lead. The basement? he thought. Why was he waiting in the basement? Why couldn't they do this outside, so the whole world could see?

He put his hand on the basement door. "This one?" he said doubtfully. He hoped Mrs. Mahoney would hear the worry in his voice. Maybe she'd come with them.

But all she did was nod. "That's right."

Owen opened the door. Mr. Mahoney was standing at the bottom of the stairs. "Come on down, boys," he said in a hearty voice.

They walked down slowly, like zombies in a chain gang.

"Nice to see you, Ben," said Mr. Mahoney.

At least it wasn't a padded cell, the way Lydia had almost convinced Owen it was going to be. It was a normal playroom. There was a striped rug on the floor and a huge couch with a coffee table in front of it. There were a few beanbag chairs, too, and a TV in one corner.

A Ping-Pong table was pushed against one wall. Another wall was filled with bookshelves.

"Make yourselves at home," said Mr. Mahoney. He waved them toward the couch. "Go on, take a seat."

Owen perched on the edge of the cushion with Ben on one side and Joseph on the other. He had to force himself not to clutch Joseph's hand.

"Well," said Mr. Mahoney. He paced slowly back and forth in front of them. Taking his time. "How was your week?" he said finally.

None of them said anything for a minute. Then Owen said, "Long."

"Excuse me, Owen?" Mr. Mahoney leaned toward him. "I didn't hear you."

Owen looked up. "Long," he said again.

Mr. Mahoney nodded. "And how did you feel?"

Owen stared up at him. He couldn't tell what Mr. Mahoney was after. But he was tired of the suspense.

"Terrible," he said with feeling. "I tossed and turned every night."

"Ahhhh." Mr. Mahoney nodded again, as if it was what he had expected Owen to say. "Joseph?"

Joseph looked up. "My stomach didn't feel so good."

Mr. Mahoney nodded again and took a step sideways to stand in front of Ben. "And you, Ben?"

Ben was staring down at his hands clenched in his lap. For a minute, Owen thought he wasn't going to answer.

But then he did.

"I was worried," he said. His voice was muffled.

"Worried about what?" said Mr. Mahoney.

There was a pause. Then, "That I was a chicken."

"A chicken?"

"Yeah." Ben finally looked up at him. "For running."

The silence in the room was deafening.

"Well, I think you can put your mind to rest on that score, Ben," said Mr. Mahoney. "You're definitely not a chicken. Coming back here with Owen and Joseph today wasn't an easy thing to do, was it?"

Ben shook his head.

"Brave things usually aren't," said Mr. Mahoney. He looked at Owen. "And you, Owen."

Owen sat up straight. He made himself meet Mr. Mahoney's eyes.

"You could have told me who the other boys were, but you didn't. I respect that. And you didn't try to make any excuses for yourself. I respect that, too."

Owen's heart was beating against his chest so hard he was sure they could all hear it.

Joseph was last.

"As for you, Joseph, you came back to support a friend," said Mr. Mahoney. "That was a very brave thing to do. I bet Owen will never forget it."

"I won't," said Owen.

They were all quiet. It felt good, having Mr. Mahoney say nice things about them. And not yelling. But there was still one thing on their minds.

Their punishment.

"I guess there's only one thing left to do," said Mr. Mahoney. He went over to the Ping-Pong table and picked up three paddles.

He came back and held them out to the boys.

"Pick your paddle," he said.

7

Trapped Again

"He *hit* you?" said Lydia.

"Are you joking?" Owen tossed his bike helmet into the basket by the kitchen door. "We played Ping-Pong."

"Ping-Pong?" This shocked her even more. "That's what he did to punish you? He made you play Ping-Pong?"

"And he gave us soda and chips . . ." Owen plunked down on a chair. "It was fun."

"You spy on the guy and he throws you a *party?*" Now Lydia was outraged. "That's the most ridiculous thing I ever heard of!"

"I think what Mr. Mahoney did to punish them, Lydia, was to make them wait for a week," said Mr. Foote. He looked up from the cutting board where he was chopping onions for stir-fry.

"I think Owen would tell you that was quite a bit of punishment."

"Big deal," Lydia said rudely. "Didn't he say anything about *spying* on him?" she asked Owen.

"Not in words."

"What do you mean, not in words? How else could he do it?"

"I must say, I have gained even more respect for Marty Mahoney," said their mom. She came out of the pantry and put the wok on the stove. When Mr. Foote did the chopping, she did the cooking. "I think the way he handled this was wonderful."

"I don't get it." Lydia was looking from one parent to the other in disbelief. "Owen does a really dumb thing, and when he gets caught, he gets to play Ping-Pong and drink soda. And you two think it's wonderful?"

"Do you mind if I go upstairs?" Owen said.

"Go ahead," said his mom. "I bet you're tired."

"I'm exhausted."

"What are you going to do the *next* time he does something dumb?" Lydia said as he left the room. "Take him to Bermuda?"

Owen dragged himself up the stairs and into his room. He fell across his bed and closed his eyes.

He couldn't even begin to explain to Lydia about how much he'd learned from Mr. Mahoney's brand of punishment. He had gone to the Mahoneys' feeling so terrified. And he had left there feeling so great.

Mr. Mahoney hadn't said a word about the spying, because this whole thing hadn't really *been* about spying, Owen realized. It had been about facing up to things.

Either you did or you didn't.

If you did, then whatever it was you had done was over. You could move on.

If you didn't, it would never be over. It would always be there, nagging at you.

It wasn't the kind of thing Owen could put into words. Especially not to Lydia. He knew it would come out sounding dumb.

But it wasn't dumb. It was right.

Owen got up and looked at his face in the mirror. Did he look a little more mature, or was that dirt?

He rubbed at the space between his eyes.

Okay, so he looked the same. But he *felt* more mature.

And all of a sudden, he wasn't the least bit tired. Maybe he'd make his salamanders a new environment this afternoon, he thought, bending down to peer into his aquarium. Go into the woods and find some fresh moss.

Maybe get a bigger stick for them to climb on.

Owen opened his drawer and rummaged around for his Swiss Army knife. He'd ask his mom if Joseph and Ben could come over tomorrow. Maybe they could start a new club. The "Men of Steel" club. Instead of spying, they could make

up a new secret code and send important mes-
sages back and forth.

They wouldn't need walkie-talkies for that.
Ben said his dad had taken them away from him,
anyway.

Owen shoved his knife in his back pocket and
put on his fishing vest. It was funny, the way things
had changed because of this. He had started off
trusting Anthony and not trusting Ben.

Now it was the other way around.

* * *

One last chocolate chip cookie. Owen lifted up the
lid of the cookie jar as noiselessly as he could and
put it on the counter.

So what if he had already brushed his teeth and
was supposed to be in bed? Which was worse:
sleeping with chocolate-covered teeth or going to
bed without one final cookie?

He had his hand on a big fat one when he
heard them coming. Owen didn't even think. He
dropped the cookie, ducked into the broom closet,
and shut the door. He barely caught the mop
before it hit the floor.

He heard his mom and dad come into the kitchen.

"Decaf coffee or tea?" said his mom.

Someone turned on the water.

"Tea would be great."

Owen heard the click of the gas stove being turned on. Then a pot being put on the burner. He slid down into a crouched position against the wall.

He couldn't believe it. Here he was, Mr. Maturity, trapped again. It served him right that his parents were talking about some really boring stuff. Like what some student of his dad's had said at college. And when the last time was they had the septic tank cleaned.

Then he heard his mom say his name.

"I think Owen learned a lot from this whole experience, don't you?"

"Oh, yes. I'm sure he'll never spy on anyone again."

"Oh, I know you're right."

Their voices sounded stiff and loud. As though they were actors reading their lines for the first time.

"Maybe we should buy him a present as a reward," said his mom.

Owen's ears perked up.

"I think you're right," said his dad. "I was thinking along the lines of a dirt bike."

A dirt bike!

Owen shot up so fast his head crashed into the

bottom shelf. He covered it with his hands as his mom's gardening boots, a plastic bucket, a basket of rags, and about twenty empty coffee cans fell around him.

There was a deafening silence in the kitchen.

Owen sat there, astounded. And then he rallied. Nope. There was no way he was going to sit here once again, waiting to be discovered. He was going to meet this head-on, with dignity.

He scrambled to his feet and flung open the broom closet door. He saw the chocolate chip cookie in pieces on the floor and the lid of the cookie jar on the counter.

"Hi!" he said, smiling brightly. "I couldn't help but overhear. Did someone say something about a dirt bike?"